FOREST
OF
FAITH

An Easter Gift from JESUS

His LOVE Lifts Us Up

by Susan Jones

Illustrated by Lee Holland

Good Books

New York, New York

Springtime buds are blooming.
Grass begins to sprout.
The Easter festival is almost here!

Little Owl glides through the air. She loops, and swoops, and hoots her way down to the forest below. Her friends are waiting— it's time to celebrate!

"Easter is a gift to us from Jesus," explains Badger.

"Well, maybe we should get Him a gift in return! That's what good friends do," says Little Bunny.

The *forest* animals chitter and chatter. "What about a hot air balloon?" hoots Owl. "A balloon so beautiful, and one that will *fly* so high, He'll know we're His best friends!"

They nod in approval. Badger nudges everyone on their way, with each creature given a special task in the making of the Easter balloon.

Little Raccoon collects flowers. Little Owl brings sticks for the basket.

Little Fox and Little Bunny hop and prance together with the canvas for the balloon in tow. They're ready to make the best balloon ever!

"This rope is all tangled!" shouts Little Mouse.

"Paint it robin's egg blue! No, pink!" squeals Little Hedgehog.

"This basket isn't big enough!"
grumbles Little Deer.

Everyone is working, but something's not right. "This won't do!" cries Little Hedgehog.

"It has to be perfect!" says Little Bunny.

"Why won't the balloon lift up?!" groans Little Owl.

Little Owl pulls on the balloon with all her might.

Little Deer plucks away heavy ornaments.

Little Bunny huffs
and puffs to try to
fill it with air.

The animals gather around the deflated balloon, feeling tired and gloomy.
"We'll never make a nice balloon for Jesus!"

"Why is everyone so sad?" chuckles Badger.

"Our balloon *for* Jesus is broken. We made it big, and colorful, and very special to show Jesus how much we care. But it won't lift off!" sighs Little Owl.

"It's not how *fancy* the balloon is—
it's what's inside that counts."

Badger walks over to the balloon and rustles within it. "Easter is a reminder of Jesus's love and sacrifice for us."

"It's His love in our hearts
that will make us soar."

With a great whooshing sound, the balloon begins to fill from the heat of the flame. The love from Jesus's sacrifice fills them with a special warmth.

As they soar high in the sky, they *feel* the gift of Jesus's eternal love.

Library of Congress Cataloging-in-Publication Data is available on file.

Cover illustration by Lee Holland

Print ISBN: 978-1-68099-569-5
Ebook ISBN: 978-1-68099-572-5

Printed in China